P.B. BEAR

The Snowy Ride

Lee Davis

DORLING KINDERSLEY

LONDON • NEW YORK • STUTTGART • MOSCOW

One cold winter's morning, P.B. Bear looked out of the window. He cleared away the mist with his paw, and then he saw . . .

. . . snow!

"Yippee!" he shouted. "It's snowing!"

Outside, the snow made the garden sparkle.

P.B. Bear got dressed.

He put on his warmest winter jumper, his socks and his boots.

And finally,

he put on

his woolly scarf and hat.

P.B. Bear went outside. The cold air made his face tingle.
Just as he was wondering what snowy game to play,
Dermott arrived. He was pulling a sledge.
"Come on!" he called. "Let's go sledging!"
"Oh, yes!" said P.B. Bear. "Let's go down the hill!"
Together, the two friends walked through the snow,
with the sledge *slipping* and *sliding* behind them.

They pulled the
sledge to the top
of the hill.
"Are you ready?"
called Dermott.
"READY, STEADY, GO!"
replied P.B. Bear.

Dermott gave the sledge a mighty push
and hopped onto the back.
Down the hill they went,
until —
almost before
they knew it —

they were at the bottom!

There was another hill nearby that was much bigger.
"Look! There's Dorothy," said P.B. Bear.
Dermott's big sister, Dorothy, was sledging
down the big hill. She went very fast.
"We're too little for the big hill," said Dermott.
"*I'm* not too little," said P.B. Bear, and he pulled
the sledge right up to the top of the big hill.

Down the big hill went P.B. Bear —
faster and faster!
He wanted to stop, but the sledge kept going —
faster and faster!
Suddenly, the sledge went over a BUMP...

and P.B. Bear went flying through the air!

He landed in a big snowdrift.
BRRRRRRR! P.B. Bear shivered.
The snow was cold.
The snow was wet.
But at least it was soft!
P.B. Bear wriggled around
and tried to get up.
The snow was slippery, too!

Dermott and Dorothy ran as fast as
they could to the snowdrift.
"Are you all right?" asked Dermott.
"That was a very fast ride!" said Dorothy.
"Yes, I know," said P.B. Bear. "A little too fast."
Dermott and Dorothy helped
P.B. Bear out of the snowdrift.
He had snow in his ears,
   on his nose,
      inside his jumper
         and inside his boots!
            "I've got snow everywhere!"
            he laughed.

Dorothy, Dermott, and P.B. Bear set off
through the snow for home, with their sledges
slipping and *sliding* behind them.

One day, P.B. Bear would be big enough
to sledge down the big hill.
But for now, the little hill
was just the right size!

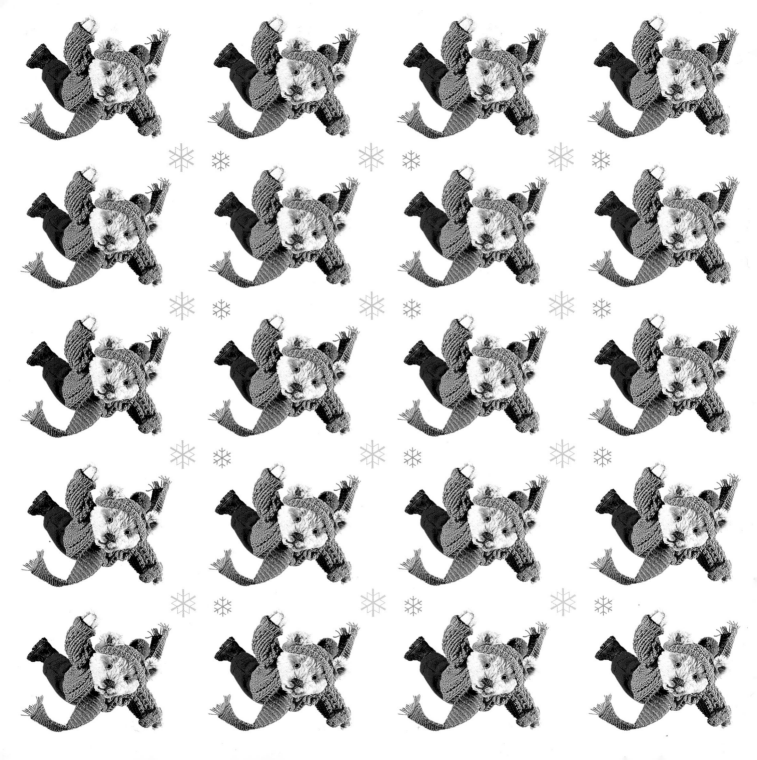